Dangerous potatoes

Acknowledgements

To my wife Ann, thank you for saving my life.

My eldest daughter Lula, the original Monkeyman.

My boys and girls Jake, Callum, Olivia and Willow
for listening in wide eyed amazement.

My sister Jackie and my nephews Sean and Simon
for Easter egg hunts in Bluebell wood, (In the day time of course).

Mark, Joanne, Samuel and Toby for help with the finer details.

Special thanks to Roger King for pointing out my over use of the lowly comma
and Sarah Kershaw for relighting the fire

This book is born out of bedtime stories.

Never stop telling them.

Cover colouring and layout Steve Cripps

Editing and proof reading Mark Webb and Adrienne Staniford

Published by Diverze Publishing - www.diverze-publishing.com

First Edition - Printed 2012 in Great Britain by Diverze Print - www.diverze-print.com

Foreword

Some children don't like soggy cabbage, smelly sprouts or bitter broccoli but, of course, everyone loves potatoes. They are just delicious chipped, roasted, mashed or fried. Unless, they happen to be Dangerous Potatoes! (Solanum Tuberosum Periculosum.)

"How can a potato be dangerous?" I hear you ask. Well, if you've never seen a Dangerous Potato you're very lucky. The children in this book weren't quite so lucky! But, you'll have to read the stories to find out just how dangerous potatoes can be!

Oh, but before you get started there's one more thing you need to know about Dangerous Potatoes. They can change nature around themselves. They can turn normal things into unusual things, because they are freaks of the vegetable world. And beware. Even listening to stories about Dangerous Potatoes can make strange things happen to you. However, the truth is, Dangerous Potatoes just want to be left alone and it's only when people bother them that problems begin. But isn't all of nature like that?!!!

The problems were only just about to begin for the children who lived in a strange sleepy little town, but for your own safety it's best you don't know where it is. No, I'm not going to tell you just incase you are tempted to go there and search for Dangerous Potatoes yourself. That would be asking for trouble. What I will say is it's a small picturesque little English town with wiggly, winding roads that amble between pretty, well-kept gardens. It's a bit of an old-fashioned place with lots of things left over from the olden days... Days which your mummy and daddy may remember. So if anything seems very old and strange in this book, just ask your parents.

Meanwhile here's a map of the town to get you started.

N
Timmy Trolley Bus' House
School
Bluebell Wood
Dangerous Potatoes
Beware.
Wiggley Windey Road
Monkeyman's Garage
Squinkle's house
Sweet shop
Wika Waka's house
Police Station. Jail

Story Six

Flashback!

Chapter 1

Flashback

Have you ever dreamed of monsters so scary you were too frightened to scream out in the middle of the night? Did you ever wake from a bad dream that seemed so real you thought it might have really happened? Well, that's how Squinkle felt one morning when his mummy woke him up for school. The trouble was that it really had happened!

"Squinkle. Wake up its time for school!"

Squinkle woke up and immediately sat bolt upright in bed with his eyes wide open. He stood up and dressed himself without a word. In fact he didn't even blink. He just kept staring into space with big wide eyes. He looked at himself in the bathroom mirror, then rubbed his hand over his stubbly head. Oh dear. He remembered now. He really had cut all his hair off. But still he said nothing. And still he didn't blink.

"What would you like for breakfast Squinkle?" asked his mummy. "You really are a silly boy. I don't know why you cut all your hair off. You seem to get more like Timmy-Trolley-Bus every day."

Squinkle didn't say a word. He just stared off into space, lifting the spoon of cornflakes to his mouth and missing each time. And then of course, getting washed and dressed took a very very long time.

Once in the car and finally on the way to school, Squinkle's mummy watched him in the rear-view mirror as he vacantly, and rather strangely, started doing difficult sums in the condensation on the car window. A couple of times she almost ran into the back of another car because she was not looking ahead.

"Where did you learn to do difficult sums like that?" asked his mummy. But Squinkle didn't say anything. He just kept on doing the sums.

They arrived at school and Squinkle got out of the car and walked into the playground where all the other children were gathered. Squinkle stood and stared at Timmy-Trolley-Bus, who was busy pulling Monkeyman's plaits. Monkeyman was angry of course. "Let me go, let me go, you're hurting," she cried.

"Let go of her you big bully!" said Squinkle in a firm voice. All the children in the playground gasped in surprise and watched to see what would happen.

"What did you say? You little maggot!" replied Timmy-Trolley-Bus, still pulling Monkeyman around by the plaits.

"I won't tell you again," said Squinkle calmly. None of the children could believe their ears. Squinkle standing up to Timmy-Trolley-Bus, (or anyone), was simply impossible to believe. But it was really happening.

"I'm going to teach you a lesson," sneered Timmy-Trolley-Bus. And with that he let go of Monkeyman and leapt at Squinkle. Squinkle casually lifted his finger and pointed at Timmy-Trolley-Bus. Suddenly a beam of light shot out and lifted him into the air. "Let me down, let me down," shouted Timmy-Trolley-Bus.

Squinkle continued to point his finger higher, sending Timmy-Trolley-Bus right up above the playground and the amazed children's' heads. Then the school-bell rang. Squinkle turned and calmly walked into school, leaving a screaming and shouting Timmy-Trolley-Bus to fall like a stone onto the dustbins with a loud clatter. All the children looked at each other in dumbstruck silence.

F= 9/5c+32
Q= mCΔT
Q= mL
Qmst
Φ=∫E·dA
∫E·dA=Pass/s.
ΣΔV= 0

Chapter 2

Our hero

The children were sitting quietly at their desks staring at Squinkle when Timmy-Trolley-Bus slumped into the classroom, covered in dirty smelly rubbish.

"What sort of mess do you call this?" demanded the teacher.
"Ugh!" grunted Timmy-Trolley-Bus, staring at Squinkle with angry, defiant eyes.
"See me after school then Timmy-Trolley-Bus," said the teacher angrily.
"Now, you can all get out your maths books," she said.
"Oh no, not maths," the children all grumbled loudly.

"Yes! Maths! Today we are going to be doing the most difficult sum in the world," said the teacher. "And if you don't concentrate you can all stay behind after school," she added. Then she grabbed a piece of chalk and started to write the longest, most difficult sum in the whole world on the chalkboard. "Now, who wants to tell me the answer to this sum?" asked the teacher.

All the children shrank lower in their chairs, as if they were trying to hide, except for one. Squinkle stood up and walked silently to the front of the classroom. He took the chalk out of the teacher's hand and started scribbling numbers down on the chalkboard. Everyone stared open-mouthed as he wrote down the answer to the most difficult sum in the world. Then he turned, handed the chalk back to the teacher and said, "Easy!"

The teacher looked at the chalkboard in surprise and then at Squinkle's shaven head.

"How, how, did you do that?" she stuttered. Squinkle just shrugged his shoulders and looked bored. "Alright mister know-it-all, let's see you do this one then," snarled the teacher, writing another difficult sum on the chalkboard.

Squinkle took the chalk and started scribbling the answer down underneath the sum.

"If you wanted to make it really difficult you should have written it like this," he said and started to write out more numbers.

The teacher was flabbergasted. "I, I don't understand, how did you do that?" she asked scratching her head. The children all started to laugh and cheer. But no-one understood what had happened to Squinkle. All of a sudden though, even as the teacher tried to quieten the classroom down, Squinkle fell to the floor and rolled around holding his head in pain. The children fell silent as the teacher tried to help Squinkle to his feet.

"You are acting very strangely today Squinkle," said the teacher. "What exactly is the matter with you?"

"I don't know Miss, I can't remember... yet," said Squinkle. "Something happened, something very scary, something involving potatoes."

Monkeyman and Wika Waka looked at each other knowingly across the classroom.

Chapter 3

Out to lunch

The school playground was full of children running around playing chase and football. But Squinkle was off on his own making something very strange out of mud. Monkeyman and Wika Waka watched him in secret from behind a bush.

"Something very strange has happened to Squinkle," said Monkeyman.

"Like what?" asked Wika Waka.

"Something to do with the Dangerous Potatoes, didn't you hear him tell the teacher?" she asked.

"I suppose so, but what could have happened?" answered Wika Waka. "And what happened to his hair?"

"I don't know yet, but he seems to be remembering something scary. Just look at what he's making," she said. The two children looked on concerned as Squinkle finished making a huge mud potato with almond-shaped eyes.

"No! No! No! Go away," barked Squinkle, at the scary potato he'd just made. "Go away, you're not real, it was just a bad dream," he cried.

Covered in mud, he stood up and started screaming and kicking the mud potato. "It's true, it's true, you're real and I hate you, I hate you, I hate you!" he yelled. But Timmy-Trolley-Bus heard what was going on. Now was the time to get even with Squinkle for dropping him in the dustbins, he thought.

“Oh! Little teacher’s pet seems to be having a tantrum,” said Timmy-Trolley-Bus as he swaggered over to see what was happening. Monkeyman and Wika Waka stepped out from behind the bush in front of Timmy-Trolley-Bus to stop him getting to Squinkle.

“Leave him alone! He’s had a very frightening experience,” said Monkeyman.

“Not as frightening as he is about to have,” sniggered Timmy-Trolley-Bus cruelly as he pushed the two children out of the way. Squinkle just kept kicking the mud potato.

“Yes. That’s it. I’ll have to mash them, mash them all,” laughed Squinkle in a maniacal voice as he kicked and punched the mud potato some more.

“Say your prayers Stinkle,” said Timmy-Trolley-Bus. He reached down to grab Squinkle by the neck. Squinkle just looked at Timmy-Trolley-Bus madly. Then, wiggling his fingers around abracadabra-style like magicians do on TV, he put Timmy-Trolley-Bus into a trance and sent him running head first into a tree. Boing!... went Timmy-Trolley-Bus’s head as it hit the tree. Back and forth he went, head first into the tree, again and again as Squinkle moved his finger from side to side. Boing, Boing, Boing.

“Ha, ha, ha, ha, ha,” laughed Squinkle. “Yes that’s it, I’ll mash them, mash all the Dangerous Potatoes. Ha, ha, ha, ha.” Then with his special magic he made the mud potato fly up in the air and land on Timmy-Trolley-Bus’s head... SLOINK. Timmy-Trolley-Bus lay on the ground with a huge mud-shaped potato for a head and all the children laughed.

All except Wika Waka and Monkeyman, who were trying to see where Squinkle had run off to. But they couldn’t find him. “Quick, I think I know where he might have gone," said Monkeyman. And they both ran down the road. 'Wika waka' 'wika waka' went Wika Waka's training shoes.

Chapter 4

The break in

With Monkeyman leading the way, the two children headed for Monkeyman's garage.

"What made you think he would come here?" puffed Wika Waka.

"To get the Metal Pants," answered Monkeyman. "If he really wants to kill all the Dangerous Potatoes, he'll need the Metal Pants won't he?" But as they walked up to the garage they could see the big gates, that normally kept naughty boys out, had been broken down forcefully. There was no sign of Squinkle inside.

"Whatever broke those gates down was pretty big and strong," said Wika Waka.

"It looks like Squinkle was here already," said Monkeyman.

"He's been using your tools and stuff," said Wika Waka.

"He's been making something and left my welding equipment lying about!" said Monkeyman. "Look over here. He didn't take the Metal Pants," she remarked and pulled on a big dusty sheet that was covering them.

"What are you doing?" asked Wika Waka.

"I'm going to need these for protection," said Monkeyman, as she belted and buckled on the Metal Pants.

"Now where are we going?" shouted Wika Waka, fearing the answer.

"Bluebell Wood, that's where we'll find Squinkle if we hurry," shouted Monkeyman, already pedalling furiously on her trike.

"Wait for me!" shouted Wika Waka reaching down to press the special button on the side of his training shoes. The shoes lit up and sprang into action sending him shooting down the road after Monkeyman. Soon the two friends found themselves at the edge of Bluebell Wood. It was starting to get dark. Of course by now they knew it was the time when the Dangerous Potatoes appeared.

"Squinkle are you in there?" shouted Monkeyman. At first, all was still and dark. And a bit spooky. But then there came a clunky, grinding sound from the far side of the wood. A sound like nothing they had ever heard before. Gradually, lights started to appear and flicker through the trees and an engine could be heard.

"What on earth is that?" said Wika Waka.

"I have no idea, but I bet Squinkle's behind this," replied Monkeyman.

Slowly, through the trees appeared a big machine. It got closer and closer knocking down anything in its way, including big trees and bushes. Wika Waka started to back away, but Monkeyman stood her ground. Eventually the strange machine, part tank, part tractor, part combine harvester, part bucket, came to a standstill in front of Wika Waka and Monkeyman. A hatch on top swung open. Out popped Squinkle's shaven head. "So, what do you think of my Potato-masher?" shouted Squinkle in a spine-chilling voice.

"Potato-masher?" said the two children, looking at each other.

"Yes! My Potato-masher!" snapped Squinkle. "I've had enough of those Dangerous Potatoes and now they're going to get what's coming. They took me on board their spaceship and did experiments on my brain," he went on. "Oh yes! But they didn't know that it would make me cleverer than I've ever been before. Oh No! I thought it was all a terrible dream, but now that I've remembered all the frightening things they did to me, I'm going to *mash all of them*! Ha, ha, ha!" he laughed.

"But Squinkle there's too many of them," shouted Monkeyman.
"Well, we'll soon see about that!" laughed Squinkle.

En masse, hundreds of beady eyes blinked open from among the bluebells. Thousands of sharp, hungry white teeth could be seen reflecting in the moonlight.

Chapter 5

Potato hunting

Determinedly, Squinkle revved up the engine on his Potato-masher and turned it back round to face Bluebell Wood. VROOOM VROOOOOOM it went, sending clouds of white exhaust smoke up into the trees. And there they stood: Squinkle, in his potato-mashing machine, face to face with the fierce army of Dangerous Potatoes.

"What shall we do?" asked Wika Waka.

"I don't know," replied Monkeyman. "Just watch and hope Squinkle doesn't get hurt."

Squinkle laughed hysterically at the top of his voice as he moved the controls of his Potato-masher. It had big blades at the front to plough the earth up and four big grabbing claws for picking potatoes out of the ground. On top there was a huge bucket for collecting the potatoes and a giant masher for turning them into mashed potato. Suddenly, the Dangerous Potatoes leapt out of the ground, launching themselves at the Potato- masher.

"So you want to fight do you?" snarled Squinkle angrily. "Well, you've had your chips!" And with that he started mashing. The machine trundled forward and flashing, razor-sharp blades churned up the ground and tossed the potatoes into the air. The big grabbing claws yanked potato after potato out of the ground and slung them in the huge bucket. "Ha, ha, ha, ha, ha," laughed Squinkle. "It's the end of the Dangerous Potatoes at last."

But strange things happen around Dangerous Potatoes. Something else was going on. Wika Waka and Monkeyman could now see a group of strange looking potatoes a little further away in the wood. They seemed to have almond-shaped eyes and were bigger than most of the other potatoes. They also had what looked like a big gun on a pod and were aiming it at Squinkle.

"Look out Squinkle!" shouted Monkeyman as a bolt of lightning flashed from the gun and hit Squinkle on the forehead.

Zapoom !!!!!!!!!

Squinkle froze for a minute. Blinking, he looked around like he'd just woken up from a very deep sleep. "Where am I?" he cried.

"Mummy, I'm scared." But the Potato-masher kept on ploughing through the wood, mashing any potato that got in its way.

"That ray-gun has turned Squinkle back to normal again," said Monkeyman. "And he's just the same silly little boy he always was."

"Yes and he can't drive a Potato-masher any more either," shouted Wika Waka.

"Look! He's heading straight for that deep well!"

Wika Waka and Monkeyman watched in horror as the Potato-masher slowly approached the well. Squinkle was unaware, and just carried on snivelling and rubbing his eyes with his head poking out of the top. The Potato-masher ambled on, as Wika Waka and Monkeyman looked on helplessly. Suddenly it was all over, as the

Great Big Potato-masher teetered for a moment then toppled into the hole. The Dangerous Potatoes followed, gnashing their teeth at Squinkle. "I want my mummy, I want my mummy," echoed Squinkle's sobs from the well.

The Potato-masher was now lodged firmly in the well as Dangerous Potatoes bounced closer and closer. They were just about to bite him on the bottom when Monkeyman's hands reached down and hauled Squinkle up into the safety of a tree above the hole. Wika Waka, hanging by his training shoes from a branch in the tree, was holding Monkeyman's ankles as she clung onto Squinkle's shirt collar. "Don't wriggle," shouted Monkeyman as she tried not to lose her grip on Squinkle.

The Dangerous Potatoes jumped and growled furiously at the three children hanging from the tree. But they were too high up to bite. Wika Waka pulled Squinkle and Monkeyman up to safety and the three sat there in stunned, exhausted silence.

"Is there nothing that can stop them?" asked Squinkle through his tears.
"I don't know," said Monkeyman. "But I'm working on it."

The children sat in the branches of the big tree until the morning came, and every Dangerous Potato had sunk back under Bluebell Wood and fallen fast asleep. Then, when it was safe, the three brave chums climbed down and wandered home to bed.

The End